This book belongs to:

Grace
florance
Picken

Written by Gaby Goldsack
Illlustrated by Caroline Pedlar

This edition published by Parragon in 2008

Parragon
Queen Street House
4 Queen Street
Bath BA1 1HE, UK

Copyright © Parragon Books Ltd 2006

ISBN 978-1-4054-8086-4
Printed in China

My Christmas Treasury

PaRragon

Bath · New York · Singapore · Hong Kong · Cologne · Delhi · Melbourne

Contents

The First Christmas

Our story begins in old Nazareth,
where a young maiden, Mary, was to marry Joseph.
But one day the angel Gabriel appeared,
saying to Mary, "There is nothing to be feared.
You have been chosen to bear God's son.
His name will be Jesus. He will save everyone."

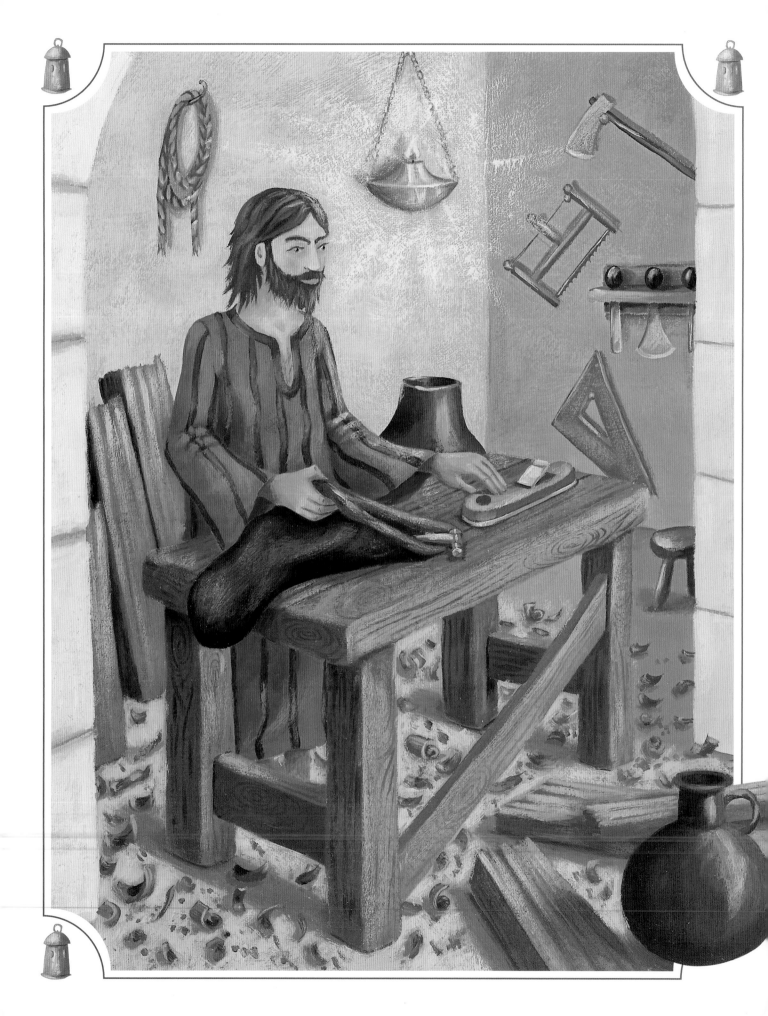

Mary was worried. What would Joseph say
if she was with child on their wedding day?
But Gabriel gave Joseph the wondrous news
that she bore God's son, the King of the Jews.
So Mary and Joseph were happily married,
and awaited the child that sweet Mary carried.

Then one day a messenger came to declare
they should go to their birthplace to pay taxes there.
Mary rode her donkey while Joseph led them
on the long winding road towards Bethlehem.
They journeyed on, all day until night,
when, finally, Bethlehem came into sight.

As they entered the town, it soon became clear
that they needed to rest, for the baby was near.
But wherever they went, they were told the same thing:
"Sorry, we're full. There's no room at the inn."
"I have a small stable," one innkeeper said.
"It's warm and it's dry, with clean straw for a bed."

So that very night, before break of dawn,
the animals watched as Jesus was born.
They all rejoiced as they saw, where he lay,
God's only son, in a manger of hay.
They did not know that the baby so small
would one day grow up to save us all.

High over the hills, on that joyous night,
some shepherds were roused by a dazzling light.
"Do not be afraid," an angel said,
"I've come with good tidings God wants you to spread.
Born on this night is a baby boy
who'll bring peace on Earth, goodwill and joy."

When darkness returned and the shepherds were able,
they left their sheep flocks and went to the stable.
They knelt before Jesus and began to sing,
"Praise be to God for our Saviour, the King."
Then they told Mary all they had heard,
before they departed to spread the good word.

In a land to the east, over hills afar,
three wise men saw a bright new star.
The wise men knew that the star foretold
the birth of a King, for it was written of old.
And so they journeyed night after night,
following the star that shone so bright.

At last they arrived in Jerusalem town,
where King Herod sat on the throne in his crown.
They asked him, "Have you seen the new Jewish King?
We've followed the star in search of him."
Herod was angry, for he was no fool;
he knew that a new king would threaten his rule.

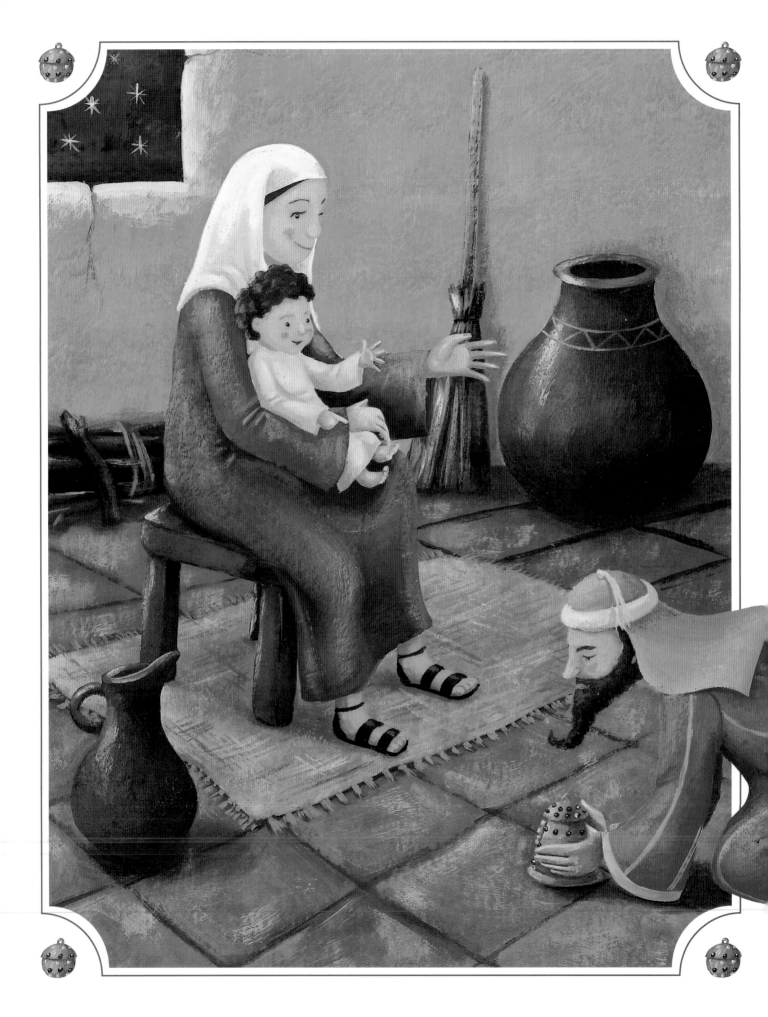

He said, "When you find the King of the Jews,
return by my palace to pass on the news."
So, bearing rich gifts, they went on to find
the little Lord Jesus, so gentle and kind.
Kneeling before him, they started to sing,
"With these precious gifts, we praise the new King."

But that silent night, as the wise men dreamed,
God told them that Herod was not what he seemed.
"King Herod is filled with jealousy,
and he means to have Jesus killed heartlessly.
So listen well to this warning I say,
and journey home by another way."

Then an angel appeared to Joseph one night,
to tell him his family should also take flight.
"Hark," sang the angel, "pack up and flee
to the land of Egypt till God calls unto thee."
So Jesus was saved to teach of God's glory,
and that is the end of the first Christmas story.

Silent Night

Silent night, holy night!
All is calm, all is bright.
Round yon Virgin, Mother and Child.
Holy infant so tender and mild,
Sleep in heavenly peace,
Sleep in heavenly peace.

Silent night, holy night!
Shepherds quake at the sight.
Glories stream from heaven afar
Heavenly hosts sing Alleluia,
Christ the Saviour is born,
Christ the Saviour is born.

Silent night, holy night!
Son of God love's pure light.
Radiant beams from Thy holy face
With dawn of redeeming grace,
Jesus Lord, at Thy birth,
Jesus Lord, at Thy birth.

A Christmas Carol

Poor Cratchit, his clerk, who worked hard each day,
asked Scrooge, "Is tomorrow a holiday?"
"I suppose you will want me to pay you as well!"
grumbled Scrooge who was stingy, as you can tell.
Scrooge hated Christmas because he was greedy.
He felt no pity for the poor and the needy.

One Christmas Eve, in old London town,
Ebenezer Scrooge looked out with a frown.
"Merry Christmas, Uncle!" called his cheery nephew.
"Come join in our festive dinner, won't you?"
"Bah, humbug!" growled Scrooge, "to Christmas Day!
What's merry about it? Now just go away!"

Later that evening, when Scrooge was alone,
he heard rattling chains and a ghostly moan.
Then Scrooge saw poor Marley, who in happier days
was Scrooge's partner with the same selfish ways.
"Scrooge," wailed the ghost, "I've come to warn thee,
mend your greedy ways, or you'll end up like me.

"Deep in the night, before Christmas Day,
three Spirits will come to show you the way."
With that, Marley's ghost then started to fade,
leaving Ebenezer Scrooge alone and afraid.
Scrooge was dismayed as he crept into bed.
But he drifted to sleep, despite his great dread.

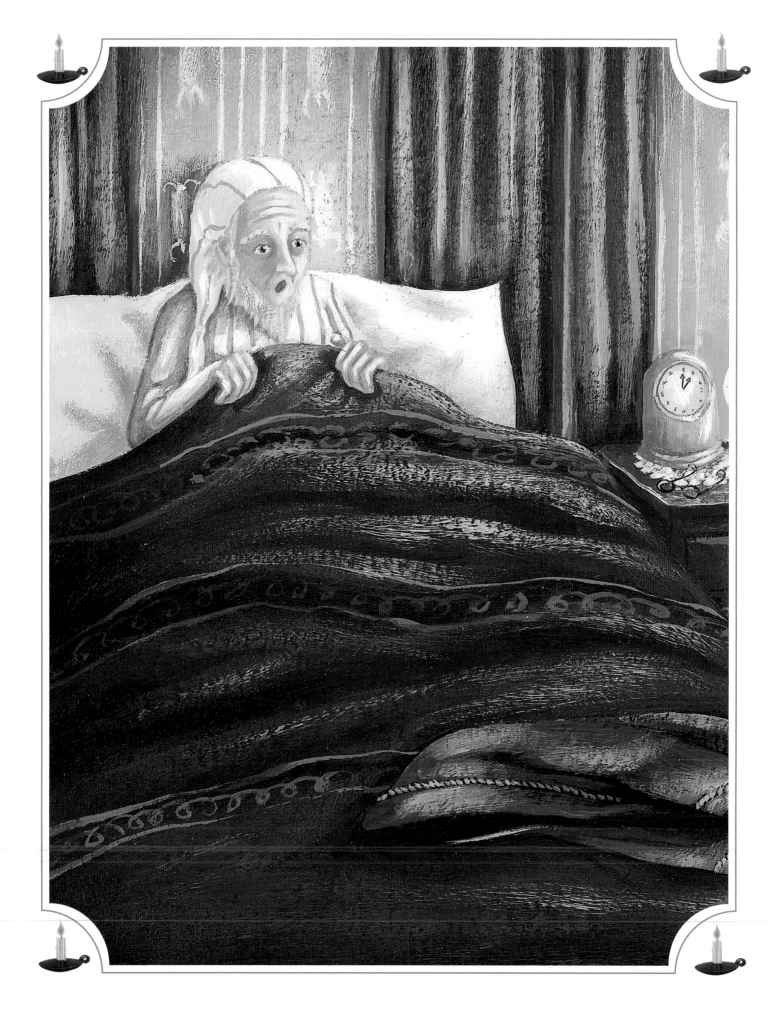

As the clock struck one on that freezing night,
Ebenezer Scrooge awoke with a fright.
And as he blinked his eyes in the gloom,
an unearthly Spirit appeared in the room.
"Follow me," it said, as Scrooge looked aghast.
"I am the Ghost of Christmas Past!"

The ghost took Scrooge back to Christmases of old,
when Scrooge was warm-hearted, not sad and cold.
They saw Fan, his sister, and Fezziwig his boss.
"I was happy," gasped Scrooge, "not lonely and cross."
And as Scrooge was shown each old Christmas day,
he cried, "I can't bear it! Take me away!"

In the blink of an eye, Scrooge returned to his bed,
and was met by a jolly spirit who said,
"I am the Ghost of Christmas Present.
Follow me now to see something pleasant."
In a flash, they were in Bob Cratchit's place,
which looked very festive, despite the cramped space.

Scrooge watched the Cratchits sit down to eat
their small Christmas dinner as if a great treat.
"God Bless us, every one," Tiny Tim cried,
as his family blessed him, smiling with pride.
"Tiny Tim," said the Spirit, "will always be lame.
But he is still cheerful, despite his great pain."

As the Spirit departed, another took shape –
a horrible creature in a hood and a cape.
It spoke not a word and seemed to be dumb.
It was the Ghost of Christmas Yet to Come.
At the graveyard it showed Scrooge what lay ahead:
misery and sorrow, for Tiny Tim was dead.

Then, handing out gifts, he tramped through the chill,
to call on his nephew and wish him goodwill.
And so began a most wonderful day,
full of laughter and joy, feasting and play.
Scrooge had been taught, as we hoped he would,
not to be stingy, but giving and good!

The very next moment, Scrooge woke in his bed.
He raced to the window, then joyfully said,
"I haven't missed Christmas – what wonderful fun.
Merry Christmas," he called out, "to everyone!"
Then he stopped a small boy and asked humbly,
"Please take this turkey to the Cratchit family."

Then Scrooge saw his own grave, unloved and unkept,
alone in a cemetery where nobody wept.
As they wandered the streets, he heard people say,
"The old miser's gone, but who cares anyway?"
As the ghost disappeared Scrooge did something strange:
he fell down and wept, "Now I know I must change!"

We Wish You a Merry Christmas

We wish you a merry Christmas!
We wish you a merry Christmas!
We wish you a merry Christmas
And a happy New Year!

Chorus
Glad tidings we bring
To you and your kin.
We wish you a merry Christmas
And a happy New Year!

We all want some figgy pudding,
We all want some figgy pudding,
We all want some figgy pudding,
So bring some out here.

(Repeat chorus)

So bring us some figgy pudding,
So bring us some figgy pudding,
So bring us some figgy pudding,
And bring some out here.

(Repeat chorus)

The Night Before Christmas

'T was the night before Christmas,
when all through the house
Not a creature was stirring, not even a mouse.
The stockings were hung by the chimney with care,
In hope that St. Nicholas soon would be there.

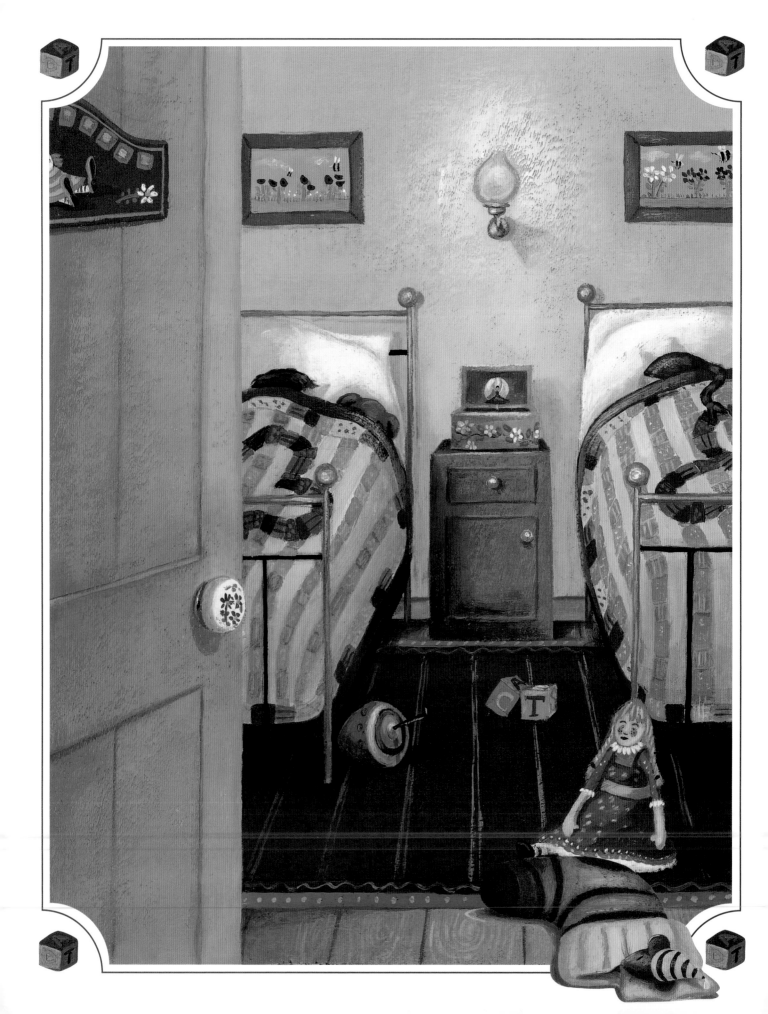

The children were nestled all snug in their beds,
While visions of sugarplums danced in their heads;
And Mama in her kerchief and I in my cap,
Had just settled down for a long winter's nap.
When out on the lawn there arose such a clatter,
I sprang from the bed to see what was the matter.

Away to the window I flew like a flash,
Tore open the shutters and threw up the sash.
The moon on the breast of the new-fallen snow
Gave lustre of midday to objects below,
When, what to my wondering eyes should appear,
But a miniature sleigh and eight tiny reindeer.

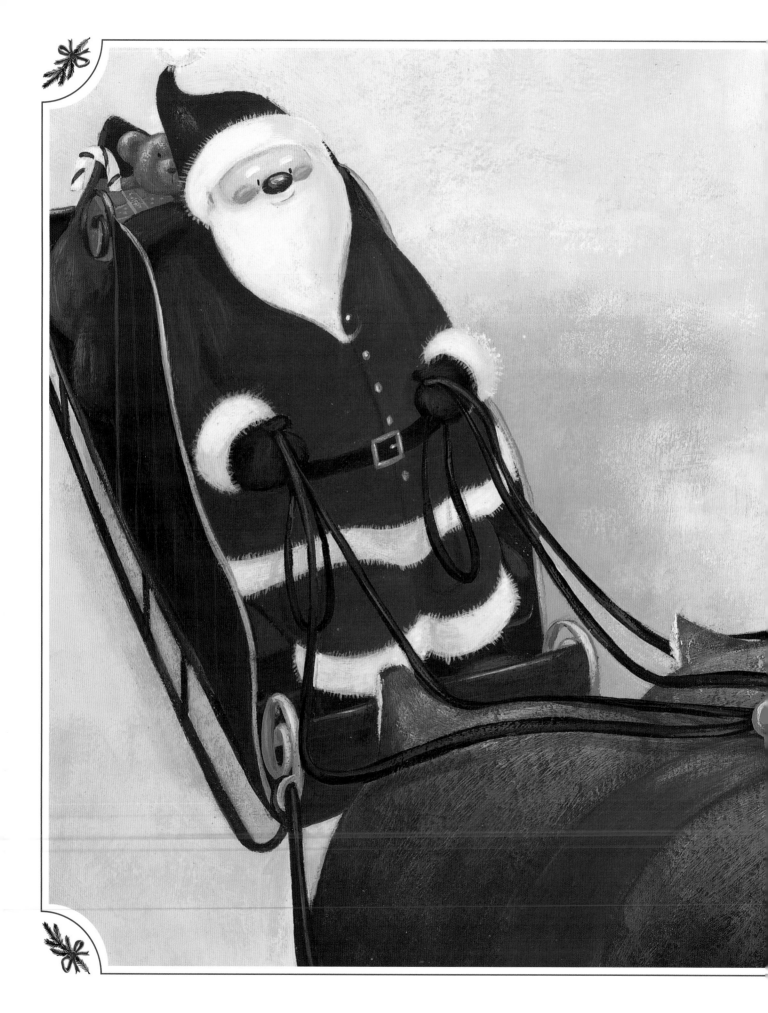

With a little old driver so lively and quick,
I knew in a moment it must be St. Nick.
More rapid than eagles his coursers they came,
And he whistled and shouted
and called them by name;

"Now Dasher! Now Dancer! Now Prancer and Vixen!
On Comet! On Cupid! On Donner and Blitzen!
To the top of the porch! To the top of the wall!
Now dash away! Dash away! Dash away all!"

As dry leaves that before the wild hurricane fly,
When they meet with an obstacle, mount to the sky,
So up to the housetop the coursers they flew,
With a sleigh full of toys and St. Nicholas too.
And then in a twinkling, I heard on the roof
The prancing and pawing of each little hoof.

As I drew in my head, and was turning around,
Down the chimney St. Nicholas came with a bound.
He was dressed all in fur, from his head to his foot,
And his clothes were all tarnished with ashes and soot.
A bundle of toys he had flung on his back,
And he looked like a pedlar just opening his pack.

His eyes – how they twinkled! His dimples – how merry!
His cheeks were like roses, his nose like a cherry!
His droll little mouth was drawn up like a bow,
And the beard of his chin was as white as the snow.

The stump of a pipe he held tight in his teeth,
And the smoke it encircled his head like a wreath.
He had a broad face and a little round belly,
That shook when he laughed, like a bowlful of jelly.

He was chubby and plump, a right jolly old elf,
And I laughed when I saw him, in spite of myself.
A wink of his eye and a twist of his head,
Soon gave me to know I had nothing to dread.

He spoke not a word, but went straight to his work,
And filled all the stockings; then turned with a jerk,
And laying his finger aside of his nose
And giving a nod, up the chimney he rose.

He sprang to his sleigh, to his team gave a whistle,
And away they all flew like the down of a thistle.
But I heard him exclaim ere he drove out of sight,
"Merry Christmas to all, and to all a goodnight!"

Jingle Bells

Dashing through the snow
In a one-horse open sleigh,
O'er the fields we go,
Laughing all the way.
Bells on bob tails ring
Keeping spirits bright.
Oh, what fun it is to sing
A sleighing song tonight.

Chorus
Jingle bells, jingle bells,
Jingle all the way!
Oh, what fun it is to ride
In a one-horse open sleigh!
Jingle bells, jingle bells,
Jingle all the way!
Oh, what fun it is to ride
In a one-horse open sleigh!

(Repeat chorus)

(Repeat verse)

The Nutcracker

One cold and frosty Christmas Eve night,
the Stahlbaum house shone festive and bright.
Twinkling candles lit up the tree
as guests arrived for the Stahlbaum's party.
Clara and Fritz both clapped to see treats
of chocolate, candy canes, sugar mice and sweets.

The last to arrive was Herr Drosselmeyer,
who offered his gifts for all to admire.
Clara and Fritz chuckled and cheered,
as two life-size dolls suddenly appeared.
Then Clara and Fritz watched entranced,
as the magical dolls whirled and danced.

Then Herr Drosselmeyer took out the best gift of all.
He gave Clara a splendid Nutcracker doll.
In his elegant uniform he was a fine sight,
And Clara's eyes opened wide with delight.
But before Clara's thanks had even been spoken,
Fritz grabbed the doll and it was broken!

Herr Drosselmeyer, being kindly and good,
tried mending the Nutcracker's splintered wood.
Then after much feasting, dancing and play,
Herr Drosselmeyer left on his sleigh.
As they waved goodnight, Clara's mother said,
"Hurry now, children, it's time for bed."

Later that night, as the silent house slept,
Clara rose from her bed and down the stairs crept.
Then among all the presents she quickly sought
the Nutcracker that Herr Drosselmeyer brought.
Snuggling down with the doll at her chest,
she waited for sweet dreams to fill her night's rest.

Before very long she awoke with a fright,
startled by strange sounds in the still night.
Sitting up quickly and blinking her eyes,
she saw that the toys had grown to life size!
Her beloved Nutcracker stood mighty and tall,
when she stood beside him, Clara felt small.

Behind him tin soldiers stood in a row
with their swords all drawn and ready to go.
Then a troop of grey mice marched into the room
and started a battle by the light of the moon.
The mighty mouse army, led by the Mouse King,
bombarded the soldiers and looked set to win.

The Nutcracker commanded as best he could,
but they were outnumbered – it didn't look good.
When the Nutcracker fell, Clara took up her shoe,
and aimed at the Mouse King, then desperately threw.
The soldiers all cheered as the King was struck down.
The mice were defeated and the toys seized his crown.

When Clara looked into the Nutcracker's eyes
she was amazed, and gasped with surprise.
For during the battle, or perhaps even since,
he had changed from a doll to a handsome young prince!
Now the prince looked at Clara, bowed down and cried,
"Come, my dear Clara, let's go outside!"

The prince led Clara to a magical sleigh
that flew through the night to a land far away.
There, beneath the stars twinkling bright,
enchanted snowflakes danced through the night.
"The dance is for you," the handsome prince said.
"But we mustn't stop here, there's more fun ahead."

They journeyed on to the Kingdom of Sweets,
a land full of dancing and sugary treats.
The Sugar Plum Fairy, so dainty and nice,
danced especially for Clara on a stage of ice.
Next came a dance from the sweets of the world,
who made Clara dizzy as they twisted and twirled.

The next thing she knew, Clara was awoken
and her Nutcracker doll was no longer broken.
Had her adventure been all that it seemed,
or was it a fantasy she had just dreamed?
Clara's questions were soon chased away
as Fritz wished her a Merry Christmas Day!

Twinkle, Twinkle Little Star

Twinkle, twinkle little star,
How I wonder what you are,
Up above the world so high
Like a diamond in the sky.
Twinkle, twinkle little star,
How I wonder what you are.

(Repeat verse)

The Twelve Days of Christmas

On the first day of Christmas
my true love gave to me
a partridge in a pear tree.

On the second day of Christmas
my true love gave to me
two turtle doves
and a partridge in a pear tree.

On the third day of Christmas
my true love gave to me
three French hens,
two turtle doves
and a partridge in a pear tree.

On the fourth day of Christmas
my true love gave to me
four calling birds,
three French hens,
two turtle doves
and a partridge in a pear tree.

On the fifth day of Christmas
my true love gave to me
five gold rings,
four calling birds,
three French hens,
two turtle doves
and a partridge in a pear tree.

On the sixth day of Christmas
my true love gave to me
six geese a-laying,
five gold rings,
four calling birds,
three French hens,
two turtle doves
and a partridge in a pear tree.

On the seventh day of Christmas
my true love gave to me
seven swans a-swimming,
six geese a-laying,
five gold rings,
four calling birds,
three French hens,
two turtle doves
and a partridge in a pear tree.

On the eighth day of Christmas
my true love gave to me
eight maids a-milking,
seven swans a-swimming,
six geese a-laying,
five gold rings,
four calling birds,
three French hens,
two turtle doves
and a partridge in a pear tree.

On the ninth day of Christmas
my true love gave to me
nine ladies dancing,
eight maids a-milking,
seven swans a-swimming,
six geese a-laying,
five gold rings,
four calling birds,
three French hens,
two turtle doves
and a partridge in a pear tree.

On the tenth day of Christmas
my true love gave to me
ten lords a-leaping,
nine ladies dancing,
eight maids a-milking,
seven swans a-swimming,
six geese a-laying,
five gold rings,
four calling birds,
three French hens,
two turtle doves
and a partridge
in a pear tree.

On the eleventh day of Christmas
my true love gave to me
eleven pipers piping,
ten lords a-leaping,
nine ladies dancing,
eight maids a-milking,
seven swans a-swimming,
six geese a-laying,
five gold rings,
four calling birds,
three French hens,
two turtle doves
and a partridge
in a pear tree.

On the twelfth day of Christmas
my true love gave to me
Twelve drummers drumming,
eleven pipers piping,
ten lords a-leaping,
nine ladies dancing,
eight maids a-milking,
seven swans a-swimming,
six geese a-laying,
five gold rings,
four calling birds,
three French hens,
two turtle doves
and a partridge
in a pear tree.

The Twelve Days of Christmas

On the first day of Christmas,
My true love sent to me
A partridge in a pear tree.

On the second day of Christmas,
My true love sent to me
Two turtle doves and a partridge in a pear tree.

On the third day of Christmas,
My true love sent to me
Three French hens, two turtle doves
And a partridge in a pear tree.

On the fourth day of Christmas,
My true love sent to me
Four calling birds, three French hens,
Two turtle doves and a partridge in a pear tree.

On the fifth day of Christmas,
My true love sent to me
Five gold rings,
Four calling birds, three French hens,
Two turtle doves and a partridge in a pear tree.

On the sixth day of Christmas,
My true love sent to me
Six geese a-laying, *etc.*

On the seventh day of Christmas,
My true love sent to me
Seven swans a-swimming, *etc.*

On the eighth day of Christmas,
My true love sent to me
Eight maids a-milking, *etc.*

On the ninth day of Christmas,
My true love sent to me
Nine drummers drumming, *etc.*

On the tenth day of Christmas,
My true love sent to me
Ten pipers piping, *etc.*

On the eleventh day of Christmas,
My true love sent to me
Eleven ladies dancing, *etc.*

On the twelfth day of Christmas,
My true love sent to me
Twelve lords a-leaping, *etc.*

My Christmas Treasury Song

We all love Christmas time, the season of good cheer.
Great fun and lots of treats for all, a festive time of year!
It's getting closer day by day, it really won't be long
So wear a happy, smiling face and sing this merry song:

Chorus
Ding, dong! Ding, dong! the bells of Christmas say.
It's time for stories and for song, let's have some fun today!
Ding, dong! Ding, dong! It's Christmas time, hooray!
Get ready for your favourite things 'cos Santa's on his way!

Can you see the lights of Santa's dashing sleigh?
Keep your eyes upon the stars and make a wish today!
Then soon you'll hear the sound,
the sound of sleigh bells getting near,
And when you hang your stocking up, you'll know
he's almost here!

(Repeat chorus)

The
End